Othello

Based on the tragedy by
William Shakespeare

Retold by Rosie Dickins
Illustrated by Christa Unzner

Reading consultant: Alison Kelly

The characters

Othello, an army general who has secretly married Desdemona. Known as The Moor because of his African background.

Desdemona, a young noblewoman from Venice.

Brabantio, a nobleman from Venice, Desdemona's father.

The Duke of Venice, Othello's commander-in-chief.

Iago, a scheming soldier. When Othello promotes Cassio instead of him, he swears to take revenge.

Cassio, a handsome young soldier, recently promoted by Othello.

Emilia, Desdemona's servant, unhappily married to Iago.

Roderigo, a rich, foolish man who is in love with Desdemona.

Contents

When you see lines written like this, they are Shakespeare's original words.

Chapter 1

A secret marriage

Two men were hurrying down a dark Venice street. They were Iago, an old soldier, and his friend, Roderigo.

Iago was scowling. "How dare Othello promote Cassio and not me?" he said bitterly. "I've got twice as much experience. I hate Othello!"

Roderigo nodded. "I hate Othello too, for marrying Desdemona."

Iago smiled grimly. "Let's see what her father makes of it. Look, here's his house."

What ho, Brabantio!

Iago shouted until an old man looked out. "Brabantio," Iago greeted him. "Your daughter has run off with Othello!"

"No!" wailed the old man. "I will find them, and seek justice from the Duke."

The Duke of Venice was in his palace discussing war plans when the door burst open. In came Brabantio, pushing Othello and Desdemona before him.

"This *thief* has stolen my daughter and married her behind my back," howled Brabantio. "He must have used magic, or she would never have married a Moor." His voice dripped hatred.

"Othello, is this true?" asked the duke.

"I have married Desdemona," answered Othello proudly. "But there was no 'magic' except for love. I told her the story of my life – of my escape from slavery, the battles I fought, the strange sights I have seen – and she sighed to hear it."

She loved me for the dangers I had passed, And I loved her that she did pity them.

The duke smiled. "Then we should accept this marriage," he declared.

"Desdemona, what about your duty?" cried Brabantio.

"Father, I am your daughter," answered Desdemona softly. "But Othello is my husband, and I must show him the same duty that my mother showed you."

"Now to business," the duke went on. "I hear Turkish forces are planning to attack Cyprus. Othello, you must take charge of our fortress there. Leave tonight."

"Let me come with you," Desdemona begged Othello.

"You can sail with Iago and the supplies," he replied, kissing her hand as everyone left.

Alone again with Iago, Roderigo gave a huge sigh. "If I've lost Desdemona, I may as well drown myself."

"Nonsense," snorted Iago. "That marriage will never last. I can fix it – if you can find the money."

Roderigo trotted off obediently.

"Fool," Iago thought to himself. "Your money will pay for my revenge! Cassio is a good-looking man. I'll make it seem that Desdemona loves *him*."

I hate the Moor!

Chapter 2
⊹ Celebration in Cyprus ⊹

Huge waves and wild winds lashed the shore of Cyprus. Most of the ships from Venice had arrived safely – but Othello's was missing, delayed by the storm.

Desdemona waited anxiously. When Othello finally appeared, she rushed into his arms.

If after every tempest come such calms,
May the winds blow
till they have wakened death!

Othello turned to his troops. "Good news," he announced. "All the Turkish ships sank in the storm, and I am married! Let there be dancing and feasting and bonfires tonight, to celebrate."

"Time to make trouble," thought Iago slyly. "Now, where's Cassio?"

Iago found Cassio on his way to the fort. "Have some wine with me," he said.

"Not tonight," replied Cassio. "I've a poor head for drink."

"Nonsense," persisted Iago. "It's a special occasion."

"Just one then," agreed Cassio, allowing Iago to pull him into a nearby tavern.

And let the canakin clink...
then let a soldier drink!

Each time Cassio tried to put down his glass, Iago filled it for another toast. "To General Othello!"

Eventually Cassio staggered off in the direction of the fort.

"Cassio would be a great officer," Iago remarked loudly to everyone around him. "If only he wasn't such a drunkard."

There were shouts in the street outside. On Iago's instructions, Roderigo had insulted Cassio. Then Roderigo ran into the tavern, with Cassio in hot pursuit.

"Stop," laughed a soldier, catching Cassio's arm. "You're drunk."

"*Drunk?*" roared Cassio, waving his fists. "I'll give you drunk!"

Iago smiled as they began to fight. "Time to fetch Othello," he thought.

Othello was furious to find his soldiers brawling in public. "Stop!" he bellowed. "Iago, tell me – who started this?"

Iago pretended to hesitate.

"I won't blame Cassio... he must have been provoked."

Othello nodded curtly. "Cassio, you are no longer my officer!" And with that, he left.

Reputation, reputation, reputation! Oh, I have lost my reputation!

Cassio bowed his head in despair.

Iago put an arm around him. "Othello will forgive you if you ask."

"I couldn't," sighed Cassio.

"Then get Desdemona to ask," suggested Iago. "Othello would do anything for her."

"I will," nodded Cassio. "Thank you, honest Iago."

Iago watched Cassio go with a cruel smile. "Of course Desdemona will help, out of the goodness of her heart," he sneered. "But I'll tell Othello it's because she's in love with Cassio!"

So will I... out of her own goodness make the net that shall enmesh them all.

Chapter 3
—+ A lost handkerchief +—

The next morning, Cassio told
Desdemona his troubles. She listened
gravely before answering. "Good Cassio, I'll
do everything I can. Look, here comes my
husband with Iago. I'll talk to him now."

"Was that Cassio?" asked Othello, as someone darted away.

"Surely not," said Iago. "Cassio would never steal away so guiltily."

"My lord," cried Desdemona, coming up with a kiss. "Will you forgive Cassio? Call him back."

"Soon, my sweet," laughed Othello. "Anything for you! But now, I must work."

With a smile, Desdemona went.

Oh, I do love her! And when I love her not, chaos is come again.

Iago cleared his throat. "Does Cassio know Desdemona well?" he began.

"Yes, he carried messages between us before we were married," replied Othello.

"Indeed!" exclaimed Iago.

"What of it?" said Othello, frowning.

Iago shook his head doubtfully. "I'd better not say. I might be wrong and I don't want to make you jealous of your wife.

"Beware, my lord, of jealousy.
It is the green-eyed monster."

"My wife is virtuous," warned Othello. "I won't doubt her without proof."

"I've no proof," said Iago. "But she deceived her father, so she may deceive you! Take my advice, see what happens with Cassio. If she pleads too strongly..." He gave Othello a sly look, then strode off.

Othello clutched his head. "I won't believe it!"

"What's the matter?" asked Desdemona, coming in.

"My head hurts," he snapped.

"Let me bind it," she offered, holding out her handkerchief.

He pushed it away impatiently and seized her hand. "Come, let's go and eat."

The handkerchief lay forgotten on the floor, until Emilia found it. "My husband asked me to steal this," she muttered, picking it up. "Oh Iago," she called. "I have something for you!"

"I have something too," he sneered, looking in. "A foolish wife!"

"Is that so?" snapped Emilia. "Well, what about this?"

She waved the handkerchief at Iago. His eyes gleamed as he snatched it.

"Why do you want it?" asked Emilia.

"None of your business," growled Iago. But inwardly, he was grinning. "This is my proof," he thought. "I'll drop it in Cassio's room. The Moor is already jealous. When he sees Cassio with Desdemona's handkerchief, his blood will burn."

Chapter 4
⊹ Othello's proof ⊹

Othello glared at Iago. "Give me proof that Desdemona has betrayed me," he said. "Or feel my anger!"

"World, take note," sighed Iago. "This is my reward for being honest!"

Othello rubbed his eyes. "By the world, I think my wife is honest, and think she is not. I think you are right, and think you are not. I must have *proof*."

"Last night, I heard Cassio moan in his sleep – *sweet Desdemona, let us hide our love!*" said Iago. "And does she have a handkerchief embroidered with strawberries?"

"My first gift to her," groaned Othello.

"I saw Cassio use a handkerchief like that to wipe his chin."

Othello's face grew murderous.

A few rooms away, Desdemona was searching for the handkerchief.

"Emilia, have you seen it? I'd rather lose a purse of gold than that..." She straightened up as Othello came striding in. "My lord?"

Othello took her hand and stroked it. "This is a good hand."

"It was the hand which gave away my heart," she said softly. "Now, will you call for Cassio?"

"First lend me your handkerchief," said Othello. "The one I gave you."

"I don't have it on me," she said.

"That's bad," growled Othello. "It has magic in it. If it is lost or given away, terrible things will follow. Bring it to me!"

"Why do you speak so roughly?" whispered Desdemona. Then she laughed. "You're trying to distract me. It won't work. Please, call Cassio!"

"The handkerchief!" roared Othello, storming out.

"Othello seems jealous," said Emilia
wonderingly. "But why?" A footstep made
her look up. "Iago!"

"What's the matter?" asked Iago, full of
pretend concern. So Desdemona explained.

"I'll talk to Othello," he offered, when
she finished. "Perhaps something else has
upset him."

"I hope you're right," thought Emilia.

Meanwhile, Cassio was showing the handkerchief to a girl he knew. "Look Bianca, isn't it pretty?"

"A woman's handkerchief!" Bianca pouted. "I suppose it was a gift from your *girlfriend*."

"No, I found it," Cassio laughed. "Can you make a copy for me?"

"All right," agreed Bianca. "But only if you promise to visit me soon!" She blew Cassio a kiss and danced away.

Othello was watching their exchange from his window, a wild look in his eye. "Look," he croaked to Iago. "Cassio's got the handkerchief!"

Iago nodded. "I suppose Desdemona gave it to him."

"What else did she *give* him?" asked Othello, in a strangled voice.

"Um," said Iago, pretending to hesitate. "What if I had seen Cassio kiss her? Or heard him blab about what they've done?"

"What did he say?" growled Othello. "Is it possible – did he confess?"

Iago nodded. "In every detail."

Othello clutched his head.

confess – handkerchief – oh devil!

"My lord, are you all right? Listen, I know a way you can hear it for yourself. Just hide up here..."

"Cassio," Iago shouted, running down into the street. "How are things going with Desdemona?" He sidled closer and hissed softly, so no one else heard: "Now if it was Bianca, things would move more swiftly!"

Cassio laughed at Bianca's name. "Poor thing! I think she loves me."

"How dare he laugh at Desdemona?" fumed Othello in his hiding place.

Ha, ha, ha.

"She says you will marry her," Iago continued. "Is that true?"

Still thinking of Bianca, Cassio laughed even harder. "I'm not going to marry her. She made it up. She's such a flirt, always calling me 'dear Cassio' and flinging her arms around me!" He strode off, chuckling to himself.

When Iago returned, Othello was ranting like a lunatic. "I'll kill Cassio! And Desdemona! My heart is turned to stone. I'll poison her." Then he imagined her dead and his face softened. "Oh Iago, the pity of it!"

"Strangle her tonight," urged Iago coldly. "I'll see to Cassio."

Chapter 5
⊹ Murder in Cyprus ⊹

Othello strode into the fort to find his officers and Desdemona gathered around a messenger from Venice named Lodovico.

"Greetings," said Lodovico. "The duke has sent me to bring Othello home. Cassio can take care of the fort. How is he?"

Othello shrugged.

"My lord and Cassio have fallen out," explained Desdemona sadly.

As she spoke Cassio's name, something in Othello snapped. "Out of my sight!" he snarled, striking her.

Desdemona clutched her stinging cheek and left, her eyes brimming.

"So *Cassio* has my place," snorted Othello. He strode away, muttering oddly.

"Has he lost his mind?" exclaimed Lodovico, staring after him.

Goats and monkeys!

Othello had gone to question the servant, Emilia, about Desdemona's meetings with Cassio. "You never saw anything suspicious?"

Emilia shook her head. "No, nor heard nor suspected anything," she insisted. "Desdemona is a faithful wife."

If she is not honest, chaste and true, there's no man happy.

But her words fell on deaf ears. "Bring her here," Othello ordered.

"You called for me, my lord?" said Desdemona softly, coming in.

Othello stared into her clear blue eyes. "What *are* you?"

She gazed back at him. "Your true and loyal wife, heaven knows."

"Heaven knows you are false!"

"How?" she begged. "What is my sin?"

"Aren't you a harlot?"

"*No!*" cried Desdemona, shocked.

For a moment, Othello almost believed her. Then he remembered Iago's sneers and Cassio's laughter. "I'm *sorry*," he spat, his words dripping sarcasm. "I thought you were that harlot who married Othello!" And he stormed out.

Desdemona wept.

"What's all this?" said Iago, looking in.

"My lord called her a *harlot*!" exclaimed
Emilia. "Did she give up her family, friends
and country, to be called such names?"

Iago did his best to look surprised.
"Why?" he asked.

Desdemona shook her head. "Heaven
knows," she sniffed.

"I bet my life some knave has been telling lies," put in Emilia. "May he be hanged for it!"

"Quiet, fool," snarled Iago. He turned to Desdemona. "I expect something else has upset him and he's taking it out on you. Don't cry. All will be well."

Desdemona and Emilia had barely left when Roderigo came running in. "Iago," he snapped. "I've given you enough jewels to win any girl, and you say Desdemona will meet me – but she never comes."

"Very well," sighed Iago.

"It is NOT very well," howled Roderigo. "She must give back my jewels or I will settle the account with *you*, Iago!"

Iago laughed. "Be brave. I'll bring you together. But Othello is meant to take her home tomorrow. We need to make her stay."

Roderigo scratched his head. "What do you suggest?"

"Knock out Cassio's brains," said Iago coldly. "So Othello can't hand over the fort to him. Listen..."

After dinner, Othello told Desdemona to go straight to bed and send her servant away.

"Send me away?" cried Emilia, dismayed.

"It was his command," said Desdemona, looking pale. "Please, help me to change and put my wedding sheets on the bed." She paused, remembering his murderous stare. "If I should die, wrap me in those sheets – and let nobody blame him."

She began to hum a strange, sad song...

The poor soul sat sighing by a sycamore tree;
Sing all a green willow...
The fresh streams ran by her
and murmured her moans;
Sing willow, willow, willow.
Her salt tears fell from her
and softened the stones...

She stopped abruptly. "Are there really women who betray their husbands?"

Emilia nodded. "Some, I'm sure."

"I wouldn't. I didn't think any woman could," said Desdemona. "Would you for all the world?"

"The world is a great prize," sighed Emilia. "Anyway, I blame the husbands."

The ills we do, their ills instruct us so.

Outside in the dark, Iago and Roderigo were waiting for Cassio. Footsteps approached.

"Villain, die!" shouted Roderigo, waving a dagger. Cassio dodged, drew his own sword and thrust it at Roderigo – who collapsed.

Then Cassio collapsed too. Iago had stabbed him from behind and vanished into the shadows.

"Help!" yelled Cassio. "Murder!"

Iago reappeared holding a lantern. "What's all this noise?"

"Help," begged Cassio. "I was attacked." He pointed at Roderigo.

"Villain," cried Iago, finishing off Roderigo. He was tempted to do the same for Cassio, but too many people were appearing, drawn by the shouts.

So he melted away, grinning to himself...

This is the night, that either makes me or undoes me quite.

Chapter 6
⊹ Put out the light ⊹

O thello walked softly into Desdemona's room. Asleep, she looked so beautiful and so innocent. "I won't shed her blood," he thought. "Yet she betrayed me. She must die." He reached for the candle by the bed.

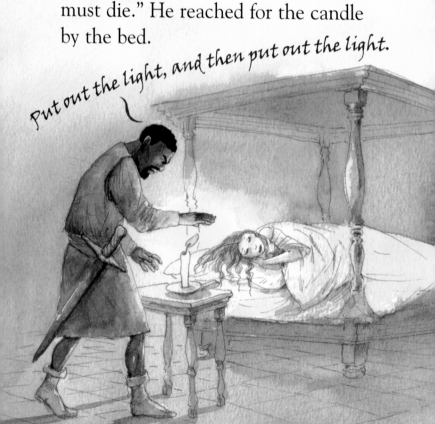

Put out the light, and then put out the light.

Unable to help himself, he kissed her. Her eyes fluttered open.

"Othello?" she whispered.

"Desdemona," he sighed. "Have you prayed tonight? I will not kill you unprepared."

"You talk of killing?" quavered Desdemona. "Heaven have mercy!"

"Amen," growled Othello, reaching for a pillow.

"I never wronged you," she pleaded.

"I saw Cassio with your handkerchief – heard him confess!"

"Send for him. He won't say so."

"No," snarled Othello. "He won't. Iago is killing him."

"Alas," whimpered Desdemona. "Let me live... let me say a prayer..."

"Too late," said Othello stonily. He pushed the pillow over her face and held it there until she stopped struggling.

Someone pounded on the door. Slowly, he stood and unlocked it.

It was Emilia. "My lord, Cassio has killed Roderigo!"

"Cassio lives?" said Othello in surprise.

"Falsely murdered..." came a whisper from the bed. Desdemona was not quite dead. "I die guiltless."

"Alas, my lady," wailed Emilia, rushing to her side. "Who did this?"

"No one," said Desdemona faintly. "Remember me to my lord. Farewell!" Her eyes closed for the last time.

"She lied," said Othello curtly. "I killed her, because she betrayed me. Your husband told me."

"My husband?" gasped Emilia. "He lies! Help, murder!"

A group of soldiers came running, Iago among them. Emilia's eyes blazed to see him. "Your lies have led to murder!" She turned to Othello. "You have killed the sweetest innocent that ever lived."

Othello shook his head. "She was false. Iago knows. Cassio confessed to him! She even gave Cassio her handkerchief."

Emilia snorted. "I found the handkerchief and gave it to Iago!"

Before she could say more, Iago lunged
at her with his sword – then fled, pursued
by the soldiers.

"I die," sighed Emilia, feeling her wound.
With effort, her eyes found Othello's. "She
was faithful. She loved you, cruel Moor!"

Othello's eyes filled with tears as he gazed down at his wife's body. "Devils take me from this heavenly sight and roast me in hellfire!"

Desdemona! Dead! oh, oh, oh!

The soldiers returned, dragging Iago.
Behind them came more men supporting
the injured Cassio, followed by Lodovico,
the duke's messenger.

"Othello, what can we say to you?"
sighed Lodovico.

"Anything," answered Othello. "At least
say I acted not out of hate, but jealous love."

"I never gave you reason to be jealous," insisted Cassio.

"I believe it," groaned Othello. "Forgive me! Tell me, how did you get the handkerchief?"

"I found it in my room," said Cassio. "Iago put it there. And he told Roderigo to kill me. We found a letter to prove it."

Othello rounded on Iago. "Devil! Why
have you done this?"

"What you know, you know," spat Iago.
"From now on, I will say nothing." He
pressed his lips together, his face twisted
with hate.

Then Lodovico spoke. "Othello, I strip
you of your command. We must return
to Venice. Cassio shall stay here to
govern the fort, and Iago shall remain his
prisoner."

"A word before you go," begged Othello. "When you tell this sad story, be truthful! Say I loved not wisely, but too well. Say I killed the one who killed Desdemona..."

Before anyone could stop him, he buried a dagger in his own chest. Slowly he sank down beside his wife, brushing her cheek with his lips.

I kissed thee 'ere I killed thee: no way but this,
Killing myself, to die upon a kiss.

Othello's hand dropped from the dagger. He was dead. Lodovico gazed down at the bodies, Othello's dusky face buried in Desdemona's golden hair, and blinked back a tear.

"This is *your* work," Lodovico told Iago sternly. "And you shall pay the price! No punishment is too harsh. Now I must sail for Venice alone."

Myself will straight aboard, and to the state
This heavy act with heavy heart relate.

William Shakespeare
1564-1616

William Shakespeare was
born in Stratford-upon-Avon,
England, and became famous
as an actor and writer when he moved to
London. He wrote many poems and almost forty
plays which are still performed and enjoyed today.

⇥ Usborne Quicklinks ⇤

For links to websites about Shakespeare and
his plays, go to the Usborne Quicklinks website
at **www.usborne.com/quicklinks**
and enter the keyword "Othello".
Please follow the internet safety guidelines
at the Usborne Quicklinks website.

Designed by Samantha Barrett
Series designer: Russell Punter
Series editor: Lesley Sims

First published in 2014 by Usborne Publishing Ltd., Usborne House,
83-85 Saffron Hill, London EC1N 8RT, England. www.usborne.com
Copyright © 2014 Usborne Publishing Ltd. UE.